The First Christmas

retold by Mark A. Taylor
illustrated by Jim Talbot

Bethlehem was busy!

Crowds of frowning men jammed the narrow streets.

Wide-eyed children squeezed their mothers' hands and pressed
through the noisy mob.

Merchants and money-changers waved their wares and shouted
for attention.

But Mary and Joseph paid little attention. They had only one
thing on their minds as they pushed through the people.

"Joseph," Mary whispered. "We must find a place to stay."

"I know," he said as he glanced at her pale face. "It won't be much
longer. I promise."

But Joseph wasn't as sure as he sounded. He had asked and
asked, but every place was full. It seemed like the whole world had
come to this little city to pay taxes.

He knew of only one more spot to try. "We're almost there," he told
Mary, as he led their donkey past a group of bearded travelers arguing
with a merchant.

Soon Joseph stopped outside a building and peered through the
open door. "Hello—" he shouted. "Is Matthias of Bethany here? I'm
looking for the innkeeper."

"We saw him just a minute ago," said one wide woman as three
small children played hide-and-seek around her feet.

"He's bringing us more bread," said a skinny man as he wiped h
mouth with his sleeve.

"He went to get us blankets," said a smiling man just inside the
door. "He has rented us the very last spot in his inn."

Just then Matthias appeared, balancing a platter of bread with one hand and holding an armload of blankets with the other. The innkeeper handed his load to the men who were waiting.

Then he turned to Joseph. "Who are YOU?" he asked in a high, squeaky voice. "And what do you want?"

"I—I'm Joseph of Nazareth," Joseph stammered. "I—we need a place to stay. My wife is going to have our baby soon."

The innkeeper shielded his eyes to look outside at Mary standi[ng] in the sunlight. "Oh, my goodness," he said. Then he looked back at Joseph and took a deep breath. "Well, I'm very sorry, but I have no place for you here!"

"But sir, you must help us," said Joseph.

"What do you want me to do?" the little man asked. "Every corner of my inn is already full. Even my stable is crowded!"

Joseph's eyes brightened. "You have a stable? We can sleep in the stable! Please, sir. We have no place else to go."

And so Mary and Joseph slipped away from the busy streets of
ethlehem and found a resting place with the innkeeper's animals.

Every night they slept close to his cow and his sheep and the
onkeys owned by all his guests.

Every morning they woke to the sound of his rooster's *cock-a-
oodle-doo*, even before the sun was up.

And every day Joseph said the same prayer: "Thank you, God, for
is safe place to sleep. Thank you, God, for the kind innkeeper and his
lp. And God, please help us when it's time for our baby to be born."

They didn't have long to wait. One night when the air was cold and the sky was clear, Mary gave birth to her baby.

The innkeeper's wife brought long strips of clean cloth, and Mary wrapped the little boy in a tight bundle. "This will make him feel safe and warm," the woman told Mary.

"And he'll sleep well here," said the innkeeper, pointing to a anger he had filled with sweet-smelling hay.

"He is the most handsome baby I've ever seen," Mary said to seph. "We'll name him Jesus, because *Jesus* means *savior,* and that's ho he will be."

The baby Jesus was crying quietly the next morning, when the innkeeper came running into the stable.

"Matthias!" said Joseph. "What's the matter? Why do you look so frightened?"

"Outside...there are men outside...shepherds....They say they want
 see you. They say they want to see your *baby*." Matthias gulped.
They've been asking *everywhere* about Jesus!"

"Well, Matthias," said Mary with a small smile, "why don't you let
em in?"

Soon five fellows bunched behind Matthias as he led them into
the stable. Their clothes were dark, and their hands were dirty. The
youngest one held across his shoulders a lamb as white as a cloud.

The oldest shepherd, a man with a stringy gray beard, spoke first.
He knelt on one knee before Mary and Joseph. "Is this the baby we've
been looking for?"

Mary smiled again. "What baby?" she said.

"Jesus!" said the shepherd. "Is this Jesus?"

"How do you know about Jesus?" Joseph asked.

"An angel told us!" said the old shepherd.

"It's true!" said the young shepherd. "It started out just like any other night. Quiet. A starry sky. Beautiful. And then we saw him—in a flash of shining light—the angel!"

"We started to run away," said the old man. "But then the angel spoke to us. 'Don't be afraid,' he said. 'Today in Bethlehem your savior has been born. You'll find him wrapped in strips of cloth and lying in a manger.'"

"And then the sky was full of angels . . . as far as we could see," said the young man. "And they were singing—the most beautiful song you've ever heard!"

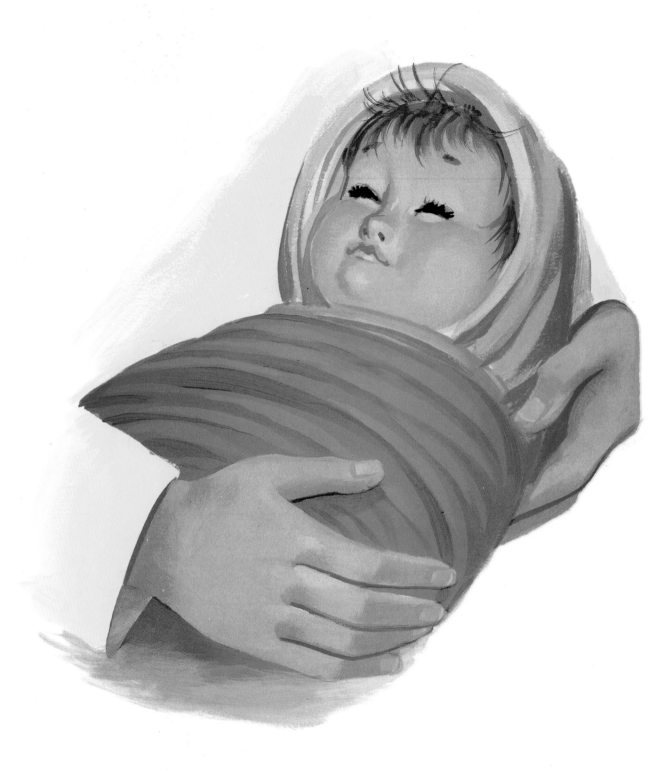

"I thought I was dreaming," the old shepherd said. "But all of us saw the same thing." The five shepherds nodded. "We just had to come to Bethlehem and see this baby for ourselves."

Mary lifted the baby so that the shepherds could see his face. "You've found him," she said. "This is Jesus."

The youngest shepherd took the sheep off his shoulder and gave it o Joseph. "We brought this for the baby," he said. "His name is Whitey. Ie's the most beautiful lamb in our flock."

Soon everyone in Bethlehem had heard the shepherds' story. Of course, not everyone believed it.

"An angel?" said the religious officials. "The very idea! Why would an angel appear to shepherds, instead of us?"

"An angel?" said the townspeople. "Why would God send an angel to a little town like Bethlehem?"

"An angel!" said the children. "We wish we could see an angel!"

But Mary and Joseph didn't listen to all the talk. They just held their baby Jesus close, and smiled, and remembered the special night when he was born.